D0324348

TM & © 2019 Ugly Industries Holdings, LLC. All Rights Reserved.

Cover design by Ching Chan
Interior design by Kayleigh McCann

Hachette Book Group supports the right to free expression and the value of copyright. The purpose of copyright is to encourage writers and artists to produce the creative works that enrich our culture.

The scanning, uploading, and distribution of this book without permission is a theft of the author's intellectual property. If you would like permission to use material from the book (other than for review purposes), please contact permissions@hbgusa.com. Thank you for your support of the author's rights.

Little, Brown and Company
Hachette Book Group
1290 Avenue of the Americas, New York, NY 10104
Visit us at LBYR.com
www.uglydolls.com

First Edition: April 2019

Little, Brown and Company is a division of Hachette Book Group, Inc. The Little, Brown name and logo are trademarks of Hachette Book Group, Inc. The publisher is not responsible for websites (or their content) that are not owned by the publisher.

ISBNs: 978-0-316-42461-5 (paper over board), 978-0-316-42463-9 (ebook), 978-0-316-42460-8 (ebook), 978-0-316-42462-2 (ebook)

Printed in the United States of America
WOR
10 9 8 7 6 5 4 3 2 1

A PERFECTLY
IMPERFECT
GUIDE TO LIFE

by Meredith Rusu

Little, Brown Young Readers

New York Boston

Contents

Welcome

Hi! We're the UglyDolls.

And we want you to know that Ugly is cool! We don't mean cold cool, like the kind of cool you feel in the winter or when you eat too much ice cream and get brain freeze. We mean *cool* cool. The kind of cool only you can be!

A lot of people think of Ugly as something different or unlikable. But that's not true at all. Each and every one of us has **little quirks**—let's call them Uglys—that make us special. And anything that's **special has to be good**, right? Of course it does! It's one of a kind! So being Ugly isn't ugly—**it's awesome!**

of

LY!

= Unique

= Awesome

= AWESOME!

Uglyville

We UglyDolls live in a spectacular place called Uglyville. And it's pretty much as sweet as it looks. We let all our Uglys shine through in everything we do here! U Buy U Break Toy Store? Check! Big Toe Donut Shop? You got it. Cookies, cookies, and more cookies? Is that even a question?

But don't be sad that you don't live in Uglyville. Because believe it or not, you live in **your very *own* Uglyville** every day. As long as you take whatever makes you special and share it with the world, then your world is, in fact, a one-of-a-kind Uglyville itself!

Every day is an Ugly day when you let the Ugly shine through!

MEET YOUR UGLY GUIDES

Now, here's the good part: We're going to teach you **everything you need to know** about becoming one with the Ugly. Don't worry; it's not as hard as it sounds. But you'll need some **trusty guides** to help you on your way. Here are the friends who will lead you into the unknown...and into the Ugly!

Moxy

Moxy is the Uglyville town reporter and is just **bursting with heart.** She knows she's **meant for something great** one day, just like she knows that *you* are, too! Moxy will give you the cupful of **confidence** you need to live the Ugly way of life.

IT'S UGLY-PARTY TIME!

Ox is the mayor of Uglyville, and he was definitely cut from the right cloth for the job. He is a natural leader and always knows just what to do, which comes in pretty handy for a guidebook. But, most of all, Ox loves getting funky and throwing a party for every occasion. (Even that time he found his missing sock in the dryer.)

Lucky Bat

Laid-back and go-with-the-flow, Lucky Bat will show you how to take it all in stride—the good, the bad, and the Ugly. He's Uglyville's resident town healer, and you can count on him to lend a wing when you're in need. He may not be able to fly because his wings are so tiny, but perhaps that's the reason he's so wise: He lives with his feet planted firmly on the ground.

A LITTLE UGLY GOES A LONG WAY.

UGLY TO THE BONE.

Ugly Dog

Ugly Dog is an UglyDoll's best friend—and he'll be your best friend, too! He's the owner of Uglyville's pet shop, and he helps pair each UglyDoll with their perfectly imperfect animal companion. Rumor has it he's also an expert rapper. Need proof? Just check out his viral music videos!

Babo

Babo will inspire you to hunger for the Ugly life—mainly because he's *always* hungry. If your lunch has gone missing, there's a 99.9999 percent chance he gobbled it up. Babo would say *sorry*, but he's an UglyDoll of few words. Instead, he'll make it up to you by sharing an armful of cookies from his cookie shop. Just make sure to get there early. He tends to eat the goods before they hit the shelves.

HUNGRY FOR LIFE.

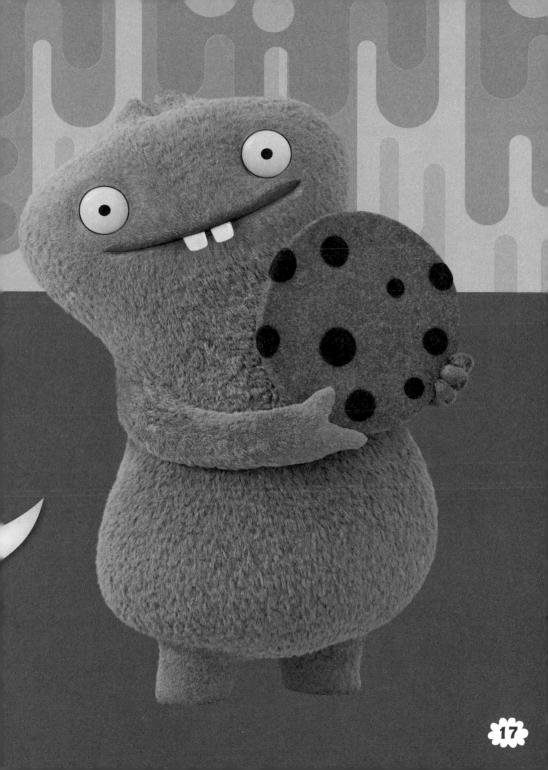

Wage

Wage is this UglyDoll's name and cooking is her game. She's the one you go to when your stomach's rumbling and you could use a chat with your chew. Wage is happy to lend an ear to all your woes. Just don't be surprised if she starts worrying about whatever you're worrying about, too. She's a lot better at handling a pressure cooker than handling pressure.

Now that you've met your guides, it's time to get down to business.

So, are you ready to be Ugly? We mean *really* Ugly? The deepest, most one-of-a-kind Ugly that makes you who you are but you never truly knew it *until this very moment?*

Great! Then take a deep breath and turn the page—things are about to get Ugly!

THE UGLYDOLLS GUIDE TO...

EMBRACING THE UGLY

Ugly & Proud

Everyone has their own quirks (or **Uglys**) that are special to them. Some of them are little things, like being really into foreign films or mixing two types of soda together to make a new flavor. Others are... quirkier. Like having a lint collection or drawing a face on your belly and making it dance.

But remember: There's **nothing wrong with being quirky.** In fact, it's those **Uglys** that make you gloriously unique! And that's something to be proud of!

Quirky Thermometer

Gloriously Quirky! →

Chilling out
in a Popsicle
freezer.

Getting Quirkier →

Standing on
your head
to watch
television.

Quirky →

Waking up at
5:00 AM to read
the paper.

"There's only **one** of you,

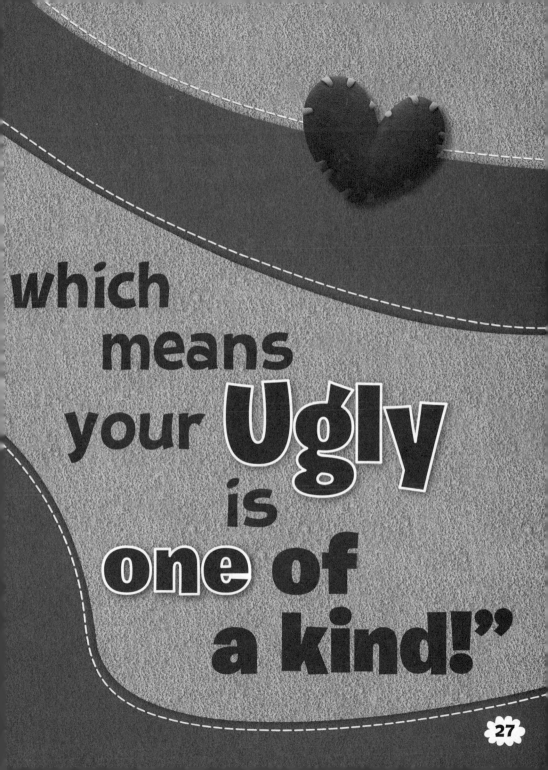

which means your Ugly is one of a kind!"

A Fresh Perspective

See, it's not about wondering if how you look or what you do makes you different. It's about realizing that **anything that makes you YOU** is beautiful!

Ugly? | GREAT!

Ugly?	GREAT!
Big ears?	So distinctive!
Oddly shaped head?	You'll always stand out in a crowd!
Smelly feet?	Helps clear the nasal passages.

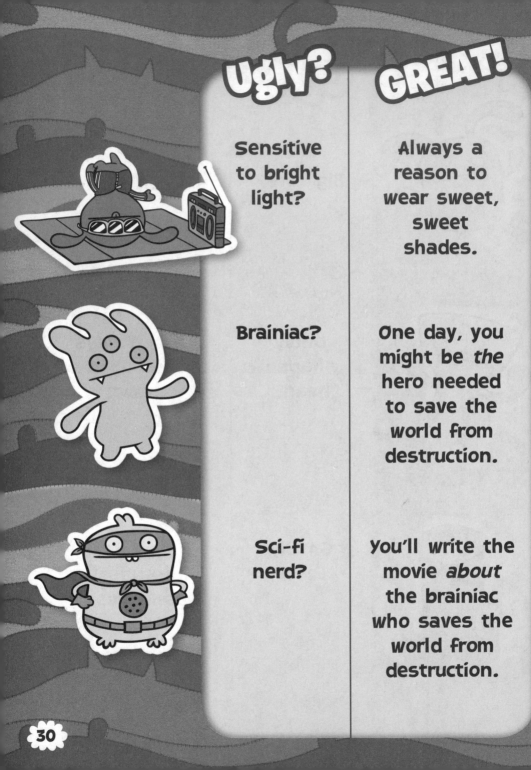

Ugly? GREAT!

Ugly?	GREAT!
Sensitive to bright light?	Always a reason to wear sweet, sweet shades.
Brainiac?	One day, you might be *the* hero needed to save the world from destruction.
Sci-fi nerd?	You'll write the movie *about* the brainiac who saves the world from destruction.

Ugly? | GREAT!

Ugly?	GREAT!
Small stature?	You'll always find your size clothing in stock.
Tendency to fall asleep in strange places?	Power-nap king!

Ugly Truth: There are no bad Uglys!

"LOVE your inner UGLY, and the world

will LOVE it, too!"

THE UGLYDOLLS GUIDE TO...
MAKING UGLY FRIENDS

UFF (Ugly Friends Forever)

Did you know there are two* types of friends? It's true! There are **normal friends**—the people who like you and will ask you to be in selfies. And then there are **Ugly friends**—your true best buddies for life.

"But aren't those just *best friends*?" you're asking. Great question! You see, Ugly friends *are* best friends—but they're also so much more. They're the people who **lift you up** when you're down, are there for you in a pinch, believe in your wildest dreams even when you don't, and, most important, **love you for you**, Ugly and all.

*Imaginary friends are a third friend category under research in Uglyville. No one can see them. But we all *know* they're there.

"UGLY buddies

are the **BEST**

BUDDIES!"

Ugly Friend Test

How do you know if your friend is a **normal** friend or an **Ugly** friend? Ask yourself these questions to see how Ugly your friends truly are!

Does your friend take your calls, even if they're in the middle of something important? Like eating? Exercising? Taking a bath?

Does your friend not only like your brand-new drawing, but truly <u>appreciate</u> it?

Are you able to be your true self around your friend, Ugly and all?

If you were going to a comic-book convention and you asked your friend to come, would they show up five minutes early in full costume...including face paint?

Would your friend judge you for eating a second helping? Or would they understand that you've <u>earned</u> those cookies?

Is your friend down to help you achieve your biggest, wildest dreams, even the impossible ones? (Which are totally possible, you just know it!)

The Flip Side of Ugly Friendship

Of course, the only way to *have* Ugly friends is to *be* an Ugly friend! There are lots and lots and *lots* of different people in the world. (More than 7.5 billion, to be precise.) But as long as you love your friends for what makes them special, you'll be on your way to making Ugly friends in no time.

Types of Friends

The Preppy Pal

The Chewy Chum

The Collegiate Comrade

 The Social Media Soul Mate

The Buff Bud

The Alien Acquaintance

The Supportive Survivalist

The Festive Friend

All perfectly Ugly in their own ways!

The Gift of Friendship

When you want to show your true friends how much you care, there's no better way than with an Ugly gift! But for a gift to be a true Ugly gift, you have to dig deep and think, *What would my very best friend who accepts me for me and makes my life complete want as a present?* Lucky for you, our guide takes the *guess* out of the guesswork!

An UglyDolls Guide to Friendship Gift Giving

Type of Friend	Type of Gift
Preppy	A collared shirt with a little UglyDoll embroidered on the pocket
Chewy	A fresh-baked batch of cookies shaped like UglyDolls
Collegiate	This guidebook. They'll love it.
Social Media	An UglyDolls filter to use on their next selfie
Buff	A handmade sweatband with the phrase *Ugly and Pumped Up!*
Alien	A plush alien UglyDoll
Survivalist	A rock. Don't worry. They'll be fine.
Festive	An UglyDolls costume

TAKE ME TO YOUR FRIEND!

"If you're true to YOURSELF, you won't

have to look far for TRUE FRIENDS."

Get Down with the Ugly

All right:
You've got the heart.
You've got the friends.
Now it's time to get
the *look*.

Life's too short to let **anything** hold you back from what you truly love. So **let your Ugly spirit soar!** Whether you're choosing an **outfit**, going on an **adventure**, or learning a new **skill**, there are no wrong choices. There's only what's 100 percent true to you.

GET YOUR UGLY ON, PARTNER!

Ugly Duds

The best thing about fashion in the Uglyverse is that there are **no fashion rules!** Choose your favorite item from each list and discover which **Uglyville style** speaks to you today!

SEW UGLY!

TOPS

Sn-*Ugly* sweater

Polka-dot jacket

Hospital scrubs

Suit and cape

SHOES

Cowboy boots

Sneaker skates

Fake bear paws

GLITTER KICKS!

BOTTOMS

Corduroys

Tie-dyed sweat pants

Denim, denim,
and more denim

Kilt

ACCESSORIES

Fanny pack

Pom-pom hat

Looooong striped
scarf

Space helmet

"LET YOUR

UG

UGLY Party Time

Take it from us—when you're living the Ugly life, there's **always a reason to celebrate**. Aced that Spanish test? *Esta tiempo para fiesta!* Snagged a great deal on video games? Break out the pixel confetti! Picked up a life-changing guidebook to living the Ugly dream? Hey, we won't blame you for busting some sweet dance moves....

LET'S GET THIS UGLY PARTY STARTED!

The point is, every day is filled with things worth celebrating. And we've got you covered when it comes to throwing a **party the Ugly way**— meaning a party that speaks to *you!*

Pick a theme that's just your style. It's your party, and you'll piñata if you want to.

Parties are always better with cookies. As in, a ton of cookies. Mounds of cookies. A swimming pool of cookies will suffice.

Also, glitter. Lots and *LOTS* of glitter.

Invite the people who are important to you. The people who care the most will be excited about the things you're excited about!

The Ugly Trail Less Traveled

Is there something in life you've *always* wanted to try, but you weren't sure if it was the *cool* thing to do? Well, wonder no more: Today is the day it becomes cool, because it's cool to *you*! There are so many ways to get your Ugly on, and there's no time like now to hit that road.

GO ON AN UGLY ADVENTURE

You'll never know what's on the other side of the mountain if you don't make the climb.

LEARN AN UGLY SKILL

Trying something new could get Ugly!

CROSS AN ITEM OFF YOUR UGLY BUCKET LIST

Or even just write a story about it. The only way to achieve the impossible is to first imagine it.

"Dive into the

UGLY
way of life!"

THE UGLYDOLLS GUIDE TO...

DEEP UGLY THOUGHTS

Getting Deep with the Ugly

There's an Ugly side to everything, even philosophy. Check out these words of wisdom from famous UglyDolls philosophers.

THE UN-UGLY LIFE IS NOT WORTH LIVING.

–SEW-CRATES

I THINK, THEREFORE I'M UGLY.

–DOLLCARTES

WHAT IS UGLY IS AWESOME AND WHAT IS AWESOME IS UGLY.

–U. G. L. YEGEL

UGLINESS IS NOT AN ACT. IT IS A HABIT.

—ARISDOLLTLE

The Beauty in the Ugly

We all have **good Ugly** days and **bad Ugly** days. And sometimes, things in life might get you down. But that's when you need to **turn things upside down** and love the seemingly Ugly in life that's actually, well, beautiful!

Wedgehead knows all about turning things upside down. She pretty much lives that way.

IT'S TRUE.

Seeing the Beautiful in the Ugly

Ugly **rainy** day outside?
Splashing in puddles is a
refreshing pick-me-up!
(Plus, you can't have flowers
without rain, now, can you?)

GEE, I NEVER THOUGHT ABOUT IT LIKE THAT. THAT IS BEAUTIFULLY UGLY!

Seeing the Beautiful in the Ugly

Feeling **sick?**
There's no warmer, fuzzier feeling than finding the cushiest **pillow**, tucking yourself under the sn-Ugliest **blanket**, and having someone take care of you.

Seeing the Beautiful in the Ugly

Made a **mistake** on your homework? *Got* **lost** during your first day of school? **Forgot** about that really important thing you were supposed to remember? Relax! Take a deep breath and remind yourself: Life's a journey. It's the mistakes that **help us grow**, one Ugly step at a time.

"Life is perf

ectly

imperfect."

Top Ten Ways to Love the Ugly

1 Don't sweat the small stuff.

2 No mess is ever too big to learn from.

3 Life is all about perspective.

4 Everything is better with a bowl of noodles.

5 And hugs.

6   An Ugly friend is always
    right around the corner.

7   One person's Ugly is
    another person's beautiful.

8   Everything is manageable
    one step at a time.

9   Today is just one page in
    the storybook of your life.

10 And tomorrow is *the*
    day your dreams could
    come true.

"The UGLY journey is the one

worth
taking."

Keeping the Ugly Alive

So you've got that Ugly fire glowing. Great! But how do you keep it going strong? Well, it's in all the **little things** you choose to do every day. Choose to be **happy**. Choose to be **kind**. And choose to be **true to yourself**. Really, the Ugly life is whatever you choose to make it. So make it a good one.

And never forget to stop, take a moment, and let your friends know how much you love them, Ugly and all. When you're all choosing to embrace the Ugly together, trust us, there will never be a dull moment.

"Ugly 2 the Bone"

-An inspirational rap by Ugly Dog

Ugly Dog is in the house

To tell you the Ugly signs.

It's time you started colorin'

Way outside the lines.

If Ugly isn't Ugly,

If Ugly isn't wrong,

That means that where the Ugly is,

Is right where you belong.

Your Ugly hair. Your Ugly brains.
Your Ugly smile. Your Ugly dress.
Just keep living the Ugly life.
There's no need to impress.
No matter what you're thinking,
No matter who you are,
Be Ugly, true, and steadfast
And you'll always go far!

CONGRATU

You've made it to the end of this guidebook. Don't you feel Ugly-er than ever? We sure do! And we hope you do, too. You're now ready to enter the world as the brightest, shiniest, Ugly-est version of yourself, and we couldn't be prouder.

LATIONS!

Thanks for Uglying it up with us. And if you're ever passing through Uglyville, make sure to stop by for a **cookie**. We'll be there to greet you with an Ugly smile—guaranteed.

DON'T MISS THESE OTHER UGLY BOOKS!